The Berenstain Bears
SICK DAYS

When cubs get sick
and stay home from school
"more work for Mama"
is the general rule.

The Berenstain Bears

SICK DAYS

Jan & Mike Berenstain

HARPER FESTIVAL
An Imprint of HarperCollinsPublishers

The Berenstain Bears: Sick Days
Copyright © 2009 by Berenstain Bears, Inc.
HarperFestival is an imprint of HarperCollins Publishers.
Manufactured in China. All rights reserved.
Library of Congress catalog card number: 2008942539
ISBN 978-0-06-057408-6 (trade bdg.)—ISBN 978-0-06-057392-8 (pbk.)
www.harpercollinschildrens.com
11 12 13   SCP   10 9 8 7 6
❖
First Edition

The morning sun was just peeking over the treetops when Mama Bear put two steaming hot bowls of oatmeal on the table, ready for Brother and Sister when they came down for breakfast. There were two smiley faces made of raisins on the oatmeal to make it more fun to eat.

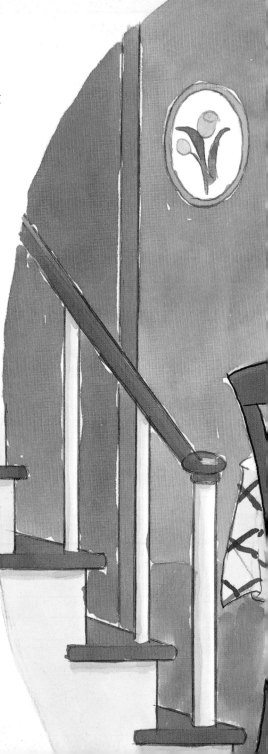

Mama heard someone clumping loudly down the stairs. It was Brother Bear, still half asleep.

"Where's Sister?" asked Mama, a little surprised. Sister was usually up bright and early.

"She's still in bed," said Brother with a yawn.

"But she'll miss the bus!" said Mama.

"That's what I told her," Brother said, starting to eat his oatmeal. He tried to get one raisin in each spoonful to make them last. "But she just sort of groaned and rolled over."

That didn't sound like the Sister Bear Mama knew.

"Papa," said Mama, "will you please keep an eye on Honey Bear while I go to check on Sister?"

"Sure thing," said Papa, leaning over his *Bear Country News* to catch some drips under Honey Bear's chin.

Mama went upstairs and looked into Sister's room. Sister was still in bed and almost invisible under the blankets.

"Sister!" called Mama softly. "It's time to get up!"

But Sister just groaned.

"Oh, dear!" said Mama and gently pulled the covers down.

Sister gazed up at her drowsily.

"Mama," said Sister in a low, croaky sort of voice, "I don't feel so good."

Mama felt Sister's forehead. It was quite hot.

"I'm afraid you may have a fever, Sister," said Mama, concerned. "I'll be right back with a thermometer."

Mama hurried to the bathroom and back again. It was the first of the hurrying she would do that day.

"Put this under your tongue and hold it there," Mama said, shaking down the thermometer. She bustled around the room, straightening up, then took the thermometer out of Sister's mouth.

"Hmm!" said Mama. "One hundred degrees! You do have a temperature. You'll have to stay home from school today."

"I don't feel so good," was all that Sister could manage to say in her low, scratchy voice.

While Mama was giving Sister some pills for her fever and getting her to drink a glass of water, Papa came in with Honey Bear.

"Brother's off to school," said Papa. "But he said to tell you that he hopes you feel better."

"Thanks," croaked Sister.

"We hope you feel better, too," said Papa, kissing Sister on the head.

"Bedder!" said Honey.

Sister managed a little smile.

"I've got to deliver an order of new chairs this morning," said Papa, handing Honey over to Mama. "I'm afraid you'll have to hold down the fort on your own."

"Don't worry," said Mama with a weary smile. "I'll manage."

And manage she did.

First, Mama took Honey downstairs and put her in her playpen with some toys. After washing up the breakfast dishes, she did some laundry. Then she went back upstairs to help Sister get out of bed and walk down the hall to the bathroom.

Honey Bear started yelling, so Mama trotted downstairs to give her some new toys. After that Mama made up a tray with graham crackers and milk in case Sister felt hungry. While Mama was upstairs, she heard Honey yelling again and dashed back down to change her. Now it was time to put the laundry in the dryer. Mama was getting a bit tired.

After lunch, Mama put Honey Bear down for a nap. *Time for a rest*, she thought.

But just as she sat down with a cup of tea and a copy of *The Lady Bear's Journal*, Sister showed up at the bottom of the stairs, trailing her blanket like a cape.

"Mama," said Sister, "I'm bored. I don't have anything to do. Can I watch some TV?"

"Do you really feel well enough to be out of bed?" asked Mama.

"I think so," said Sister, curling up on the sofa. "I feel a lot better now."

"Well, all right then," said Mama, turning on the TV. "You can watch for a little while."

After making sure Sister was comfortable, Mama went into the kitchen to get something out of the freezer for dinner.

Sister enjoyed lying on the sofa watching TV. She was wrapped in her blanket and propped up on soft pillows. She watched a DVD of *The Bear of the Rings*, one of her favorites. The sofa reminded her of the big castle in the movie.

Sister decided that her castle needed to be stronger in case the servants of the Wicked Bear attacked.

Sister gathered cushions from all the chairs in the room and piled them up around the sofa. She got a broom out of the closet and pretended it was a catapult to shoot pillows at the attacking army. She shot a pillow right across the room and knocked one of Mama's potted plants on the floor. The dirt from the plant went everywhere.

"I see you're feeling *much* better!" said Mama, looking at the damage. "If you're well enough to knock over my plants, you're well enough to help me clean up."

When they were finished, Sister was worn out. She was still sick, after all. She lay down on the sofa and took a little nap.

But Mama didn't get a moment's peace because Honey Bear woke up from her nap and wanted to play.

Mama looked up at the clock. It was nearly time for Brother to come home from school, and Mama always liked to have milk and cookies ready for the cubs to eat before they started their homework.

"Oh, my aching back!" groaned Mama, getting up from the floor and going into the kitchen.

A few minutes later, Brother Bear came home.

"Hi, Mama!" he called, tossing his book bag on a chair. "How's Sister?"

"Much better, thank you!" Sister answered from the living room. She was awake again and nearly feeling like her old self.

"That's good news," said Brother, "because I brought you your homework."

"But, I can't do homework!" said Sister. "I'm sick!"

"You just said you were much better," Mama pointed out, coming in with milk and cookies on a tray.

"Well, yes," admitted Sister, "but not *that* much better."

"I think you'd better do your homework anyway," said Mama. "I don't think you're going to be sick enough to stay home from school tomorrow."

"Aw, Mama!" Sister sighed. But she did her homework all the same.

When Papa came home from making his furniture deliveries, he found Brother and Sister hard at work on their homework. Honey Bear was busily knocking down the castle of blocks on the floor, and Mama Bear was sitting at the kitchen table, holding her head in her hands.

"Whatever's the matter?" asked Papa, concerned.
"I don't feel so good," said Mama in a low, croaky sort of voice.

That night Mama went to sleep early while Papa put the cubs to bed by himself.

"What's wrong with Mama?" asked Sister as Papa tucked her in.

"She has a little fever," he told her, kissing her goodnight. "She probably has a touch of what you had today. I'm sure she'll get over it in a day or two, just like you did."

"Poor Mama," said Brother. "She can't even stay home from school. She doesn't go to school!"

"Don't worry," said Papa, turning out the light. "I'll take good care of both Mama and Honey tomorrow. Mama will be able to stay home from *home* for a day!"

And that is exactly what Mama Bear did.